SPACE RACE

by Judith Bauer Stamper
Illustrated by Jerry Zimmerman
Phonics Activities by Wiley Blevins

Hello Reader! Phonics Fun
Sci-Fi Phonics • Rhyming Word Families

SCHOLASTIC INC. Cartwheel ·B·O·O·K·S·®

New York   Toronto   London   Auckland   Sydney

They came to race
from outer space.

A NOTE TO PARENTS

Reading is often considered the most important skill children learn in the primary grades. Much can be done at home to lay the foundation for early reading success.

When they read, children use the following to figure out words: story and picture clues, how a word is used in a sentence, and sound/spelling relationships. The **Hello Reader!** *Phonics Fun* series focuses on sound/spelling relationships through phonics activities. Phonics instruction unlocks the door to understanding sounds and the letters or spelling patterns that represent them.

The **Hello Reader!** *Phonics Fun* series is divided into the following three sets of books, based on important phonic elements:
- **Sci-Fi Phonics**: word families
- **Monster Phonics**: consonants, blends, and digraphs
- **Funny Tale Phonics**: short and long vowels

Learn About Word Families

The Sci-Fi Phonics stories, including *Space Race*, feature words that rhyme and contain the same spelling pattern. These books help children become aware of and use common word parts when decoding, or sounding out, new words. After reading the book, you might wish to begin lists of words that belong to the same word family. Your child can use these lists for reading practice or as reference when spelling words.

Enjoy the Activities
- Challenge your child to build words using the letters and word parts provided. Help your child by demonstrating how to sound out new words.
- Match words with pictures to help your child attach meaning to text.
- Become word detectives by identifying story words with the same sound, letter, or spelling pattern.
- Keep the activities game-like and praise your child's efforts.

Develop Fluency

Encourage your child to read these books again and again and again. Each time, set a different purpose for reading.
- Look for rhyming words or words that begin and end with the same sound.
- Suggest to your child that he or she read the book to a friend, family member, or even a pet.

Whatever you do, have fun with the books and instill the joy of reading in your child. It is one of the most important things you can do!

—Wiley Blevins, Reading Specialist
Ed.M., Harvard University

To Genevieve and Gwen
—J.B.S.

To Jordan
—J.Z.

Text copyright © 1998 by Judith Bauer Stamper.
Illustrations copyright © 1998 by Jerry Zimmerman.
All rights reserved. Published by Scholastic Inc.
HELLO READER! and CARTWHEEL BOOKS and associated logos
are trademarks and/or registered trademarks of Scholastic Inc.

Library of Congress Cataloging-in-Publication Data

Stamper, Judith Bauer.
    Space race / by Judith Bauer Stamper; illustrated by Jerry Zimmerman; phonics activities by Wiley Blevins.
        p.   cm.—(Hello reader! Phonics fun. Sci-fi phonics)
    "Rhyming word families."
    "Cartwheel books."
    Summary: Zip, Zat, Zing, and Ray have a fun race in space.
Includes related phonics activities.
    ISBN 0-590-76267-2
    [1. Outer space—Fiction. 2. Stories in rhyme.]
I. Zimmerman, Jerry, ill. II. Blevins, Wiley. III. Title. IV. Series.
PZ8.3.S78255Sp   1998
[E]—dc21
                                                                97-23395
                                                                    CIP
                                                                     AC

10 9 8 7 6 5 4 3 2 1   8 9/9 0/0 01 02
                    Printed in the U.S.A.   24
                    First printing, January 1998

The first was Zip
in his bright red ship.

The next was Zat
with his robot cat.

Then came Zing
on top of a wing.

Ray came last
with a big, loud blast.

The countdown
flashed in the sky.
Five, four, three, two, one.
Fly!

The ships shot away
into the Milky Way.

Zat led the pack
with Ray in back.

Ray passed Zip
with a funny flip.

He passed by Zing
with a silly swing.

Help! Zat hit a big blob!
Ray flew up to do the job.

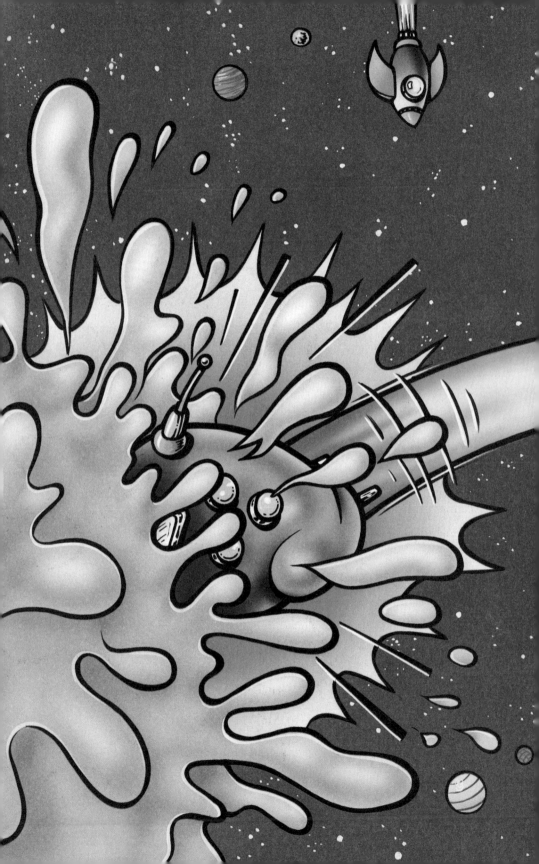

Zat gave Ray a happy grin.
Together, they flew home
to win.

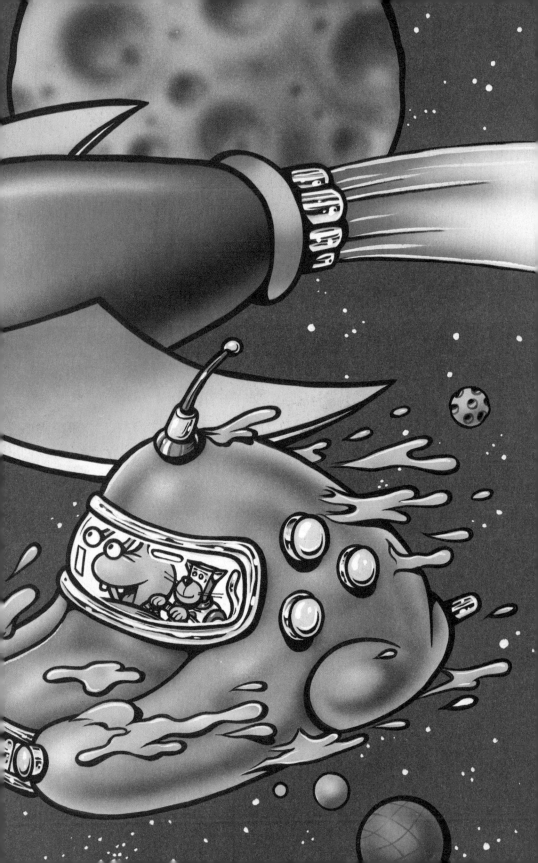

Zip and Zing
came in to dock.

Then they all had a party
that made space ROCK!

• PHONICS ACTIVITIES •
Word Families

Point to the words in each group that belong to the same word family.

flip	sad
hit	rip
lip	tip
ship	hip

bat	fat
cat	had
box	rat
sat	hat

ring	run
sing	king
wing	sit
swing	thing

Lost in Space

Help Ray find his spaceship.
Follow the path that contains
pairs of rhyming words.

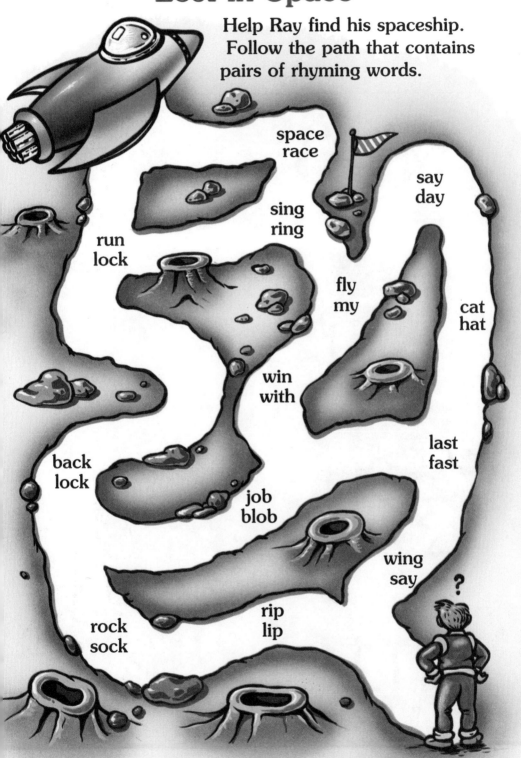

Picture Match

Match the picture with its name. Find the picture's name in the story.

cat

swing

rock

ship

Rhyme Time

Name each picture. Match the pictures whose names rhyme.

Answers

Word Families

(flip)	sad
(hit)	(rip)
(lip)	(tip)
(ship)	(hip)

(bat)	(fat)
(cat)	(had)
box	(rat)
(sat)	(hat)

(ring)	run
(sing)	(king)
(wing)	(sit)
(swing)	(thing)

Picture Match

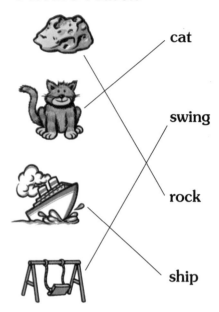

cat

swing

rock

ship

Lost in Space

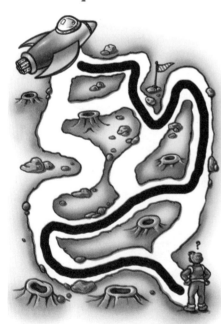

Rhyme Time

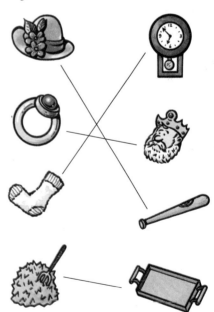